MARAMY

One Woman's Story

Pearl Ashton Talker

PUBLISHED BY FIDELI PUBLISHING INC.

Copyright © 2015 by Pearl Ashton Talker

Maramy — One Woman's Story

Paperback – published 2015 Fideli Publishing Inc.

ISBN: 978-1-60414-886-2

The characters, and the incidents in this book are entirely the product of the author's imagination though some events may be based upon fact.

CHAPTER 1

The wailing sirens of the police and ambulances, the screams and turmoil on the road. "When will it stop?" thought Maramy sadly. "Another suicide bomber causing destruction for himself and others."

Her ailing mother's loud complaints cut the air sharply. "Where are you, Maramy? I need a hot cup of tea," she demanded. Maramy sighed, thinking, "She's lost in her own little world, so unaware of what is going on in the bleakness of the world today. How she has changed over the years. My laughing, happy mother, so far from the complaining, spiteful woman she has become." Maramy quickly made her mother a hot cup of tea, and with a gentle kiss, said a quick goodbye. She walked briskly into the sunshine. Suicide bombers or no, she had to be at work, and in the light of the last few months, had no alternative but to take that now dreaded vehicle — a bus!

The day passed quickly and busily. She dreaded her homecoming and the querulous complaints of her mother. "I should get a Filipina girl to stay with her" she thought, "but how on earth can I afford it with my low salary? I'll speak to Ofer. Maybe he will help. At least he can afford it," she said to herself. Thinking of her bullying and pompous older brother and his imperious wife gave her no comfort. Her mother adored her only son but he had no patience either for her or his sister's problems. He was completely enwrapped in his pretty, selfish wife and their two equally selfish sons. "The boys don't even come to visit their grandmother anymore," she thought sadly. "How much love and attention they received from us in their growing years. Now they don't even bother to pick up the phone and say "hello." I'll phone National Insurance. Maybe they will help out" Maramy comforted herself.

As she entered home after a long day at work, her mother's angry voice greeted her. "You are late, Maramy. I've been worried. Why didn't you phone?"

Maramy answered wearily, "Mummy, I missed my usual bus, as I had to finish some work. You know the buses don't come that often." She took out the meatballs and rice she had cooked the evening before, and made a quick salad as the dinner heated in the microwave. "Every day the same routine. I'm sick of it," she thought, finding consolation in self-pity. She and her mother ate silently, watching the news on the television set, and seeing the chaos of the morning's terror attack. "Oh, God, she thought again, when will it stop?"

Her thoughts wandered to the pitiful state of her colleague at work. His only son had been injured in a terrorist attack on a bus, and had been in a coma for the past two years. Every day the father rushed to the hospital from work, and stayed with his son till late at night. The young father had become an old man within the last two years, his face wrinkled and his shoulders bent.

She thought of the young girl and her father, who were buried on what was to be the girl's wedding day. She thought of her second cousin Bert, who was shot by snipers when he rushed to help the victims of a suicide bomber's crazed attack. Bert had left a young wife and three small children. "So much pain and sorrow," she thought sadly.

Her thoughts were interrupted by her mother's shrill voice. "I'm lonely here. Why can't we go back to our old neighborhood? We were happy there. Your father took good care of me when he was alive. Now I'm just a neglected old woman, not wanted by anyone," she complained.

"I'm lonely too," Maramy replied sadly. "This place is not central and I have no friends around here. But it is all I can afford. You know that dad did not leave us much, and his pension is a pittance. What can I do?"

CHAPTER 2

On hearing her mother's words Maramy fell into a deep reverie. Memories came flooding back. The happy days when her father would swing her around while she screamed happily. The moments when he carried her up to bed when she fell asleep while sitting with the family in the old-fashioned sitting room with its antique furniture and her mother's choice of floral drapes and plush carpets. How many times she had pretended to be asleep just so he could carry her up so she could snuggle into her warm bed while he placed her pink blanket over her, kissed her forehead and returned to the rooms below?

He was a handsome man, rugged and broad-shouldered. He was jolly and entertaining, always smiling and pleased with his lot. He adored his wife and children, who were his whole life. Yet he had many friends and interests.

His parents were English and he had had an English education, so he spoke the language perfectly. He spoke to his children in English, knowing the importance of languages. As a young man, he had come from England to volunteer on a kibbutz, found he loved the life in Israel, felt he had found the woman of his dreams; a kibbutz member devoted to the land, and unhesitatingly decided to stay. It was not easy, the years on the kibbutz, but he took everything in stride, always smiling and content, with an aura of goodness and kindness Maramy had never seen in any other man.

It was her mother's plaintive complaints that made them decide to leave the kibbutz. "Ariel, I hate it here. … Ariel, Ofer is growing and will be stunted here. … What future will he have here? … Ariel, you are qualified. …You could get a job in town," and so it went on, the whining day and night.

Her father would have done anything to please his wife and keep her happy. He hated the idea of living in town, but eventually they decided to leave, and found a small apartment in nearby Jerusalem. He was lucky enough to procure a job as the chief editor of a local magazine, but this petered out when the office and press closed down because of lack of profit. He then went to work in a publishing company, but the salary was not much, and the hours were long. He never complained, never asked his wife to help out, but one could discern his discontent. He was made for outdoor life, not cooped up in an office all day.

When he returned from work, usually quite late, Maramy and Ofer would jump on him happily."I love you, dad," Maramy would whisper in his ear, while Ofer, now in his teens, was rather less effusive.

Ofer on the kibbutz was not Ofer in town. He studied hard, learnt a profession and was very ambitious. But he had become hard and cynical, and Maramy and he began to grow very much apart. He now had his own friends, and had no time for his younger sister. Maramy remembered with bitterness the hurt she had suffered.

Her mother never saw the change, as in her eyes he was always perfect. Neither did she see the withering of her once energetic and vibrant husband. She was happy with her lot, loved city life, made friends and was a vivacious and entertaining hostess.

Maramy and her father were close. He sensed her disappointment with Ofer's aloofness, and did his best to encourage and praise her.

CHAPTER 3

Maramy was 15 when tragedy struck. Her father was with the family one minute, and the next they knew he had gone. He had a massive heart attack while sitting with the family for supper. It was a Saturday night and he had not had to work that day. Maramy was sitting next to him, chattering happily about school and friends, her activities in general and all kinds of unimportant matters that still meant so much to a 15 year old. Her father was always attentive, and loved to hear her talk.

He had noticed that his wife always gave her attention to Ofer, and realised that Maramy was neglected, and he felt her hurt. He did his best to make up for the lack of interest Maramy received from her mother. He did not take sides, and was equally devoted to Ofer, and ready always to hear whatever he had to say, on whatever topic was of interest to Ofer. Ariel was a pillar of solidarity to the family, who relied on him for everything.

Maramy suddenly saw her father slump forward, hitting his face on the table. She screamed, and Ofer ran to phone for an ambulance. Her mother wailed hysterically. She relied on her husband for everything, and loved him dearly.

The ambulance arrived quite soon, and the doctor and paramedics rushed in. Too late! Maramy's beloved father had left them forever. The days following were a nightmare. Maramy was in shock, a shock she would never recover from. Her mother was lost, not believing that this could have happened so suddenly.

Now Ofer had to be the man of the house. He took charge, and many of Ariel's vast number of friends came in to help. How well-loved he had been, by all and sundry. Her mother's friends, Ofer's friends and Maramy's friends and schoolteachers attended the funeral and visited during the six-day mourning period.

Neighbors brought food; the rabbi came in daily to pray. Maramy's mind was in a haze. She had lost her much beloved father, and life would never be the same.

Ofer decided that they should move as quickly as possible, as he was not yet working and they could not afford to stay in the same neighborhood and apartment. He chose a tiny two-bedroom apartment and they quickly moved in. There had been a heavy mortgage on their old home, so they really did not get much after paying it off.

They all hated the new place. Her mother changed into an angry, bitter woman whose health failed. She would sit for hours looking into blank space. Ofer could take it no more. He finished his studies, got a good job, and lost no time in renting another apartment for himself.

At the age of 16, Maramy had to find work. She started working in a firm needing a good English typist. Though Maramy was neat, fast and accurate in her typing, she hated it and wished she could learn another profession. Without her father's encouragement she had become introverted, lacking in confidence, and diffident and unambitious. This probably prevented her from getting promotions and raises in salary that she deserved.

Her co-workers noticed her striking beauty and her youth, but she somehow seemed aloof and not too friendly. Looking back on her life, Maramy thought, "What could they know of the pain and shock of losing someone one loved so deeply? Would they understand if they knew?" So she kept to herself, speaking only when she needed to, and mostly about work matters.

Ofer was now doing well, had met and married a rich man's only daughter. They had two little sons. Maramy was asked to baby-sit often. She did so gladly, and she adored the little ones. However, it was not always possible to help, due to her office work and also her ailing mother. For five years, she helped as much as she could, buying presents for the little ones and taking them out on weekends. It was difficult to combine this with her life at home and at work, but she did her best.

Now Ofer hardly visited or phoned, and never asked about Maramy's job, her salary or her life in general. He was still the apple of her mother's eye, but for Maramy it was a big disappointment that he did not seem to care much for either his mother or sister.

CHAPTER 4

aramy was roused in her reveries by the shrill tone of the telephone. "Who could it be?" Maramy wondered. "Maybe Ofer, but he never phones on a weekday."

Picking up the receiver, she heard a pleasant voice on the other end. "Maramy, is that you? This is Kristina, the new girl at the office. I was wondering if you would like to have dinner with me somewhere? There's a lovely new garden place that I would like to visit, and I'm told the food is excellent and yet not expensive."

"How shall we get there?" Maramy asked. "You don't live nearby."

"Where can we meet?" Kristina answered in her thick but pleasant Russian accent. "I drive. I have a car. I can pick you up and also take you back home."

Maramy was sorely tempted. "I'd love to come, Kristina, but my mother doesn't like to be alone in the evenings."

"I'll bring my aunt to stay with her till we return," Kristina answered.

Maramy thought her mother would not like that, "What the heck!" she thought, "I deserve a break sometimes!" After a moment's hesitation she gave her address to Kristina and fixed a time. "What a doll," Maramy thought, "beautiful and clever, yet friendly and kind."

Maramy dressed quickly. It would be her first night out in many months. When she was ready she informed her mother of her intended outing. There was an explosion.

"You selfish girl!" her mother shrieked angrily. "You know how I dread being alone in the evenings. It's bad enough in the day!"

"You won't be alone," Maramy replied reassuringly. "I've arranged for someone to be with you. She will be here soon." She paid no more attention to her mother's mumblings and grumblings. She intended to enjoy herself for a change.

A quick look in the mirror showed a lovely face and figure, a sweet mouth and sparkling eyes. "I'm only 20. I should be going out more often."

She was a serious girl by nature, very fond of reading good books and pouring through autobiographies. There was a hint of sadness in her grey-blue eyes, but she could be a bloomer in company, her wit and knowledge together with her rare beauty making her a striking companion to be admired and respected.

The change in her mother was a blow to the young girl, and it was hard for her to face. She loved her mother dearly, and her mother had been devoted to her husband and children till the sudden death of her beloved husband. This that she always seemed to prefer Ofer to her did not hurt Maramy too deeply, as her father's love had made up for everything else.

The tragedy of losing her husband had somehow unhinged her mother from reality. The shock had affected not only her physical health, but also her mentality and way of thinking. She had become unhappy, self-pitying and self-centered, and Maramy had to bear the brunt of the change. But Maramy remembered her as she used to be, and was patient and understanding as far as one could possibly be. However, the time with her mother was not pleasant, and she jumped happily at tonight's chance to escape another dull and depressing evening.

The doorbell rang.

CHAPTER 5

Kristina was beautiful, with an aura of kindness and sweetness that filled the drab room with light and joy. "I'm so happy to have her as a friend," thought Maramy.

Actually, Kristina had sensed Maramy's loneliness and felt she had to do something to help her spirits.

With Kristina was a much older woman, tall and thin, with an austere appearance but a pleasant smile. "This is my aunt," Kristina said, smiling. They made the necessary introduction to Maramy's mother, who, surprisingly, seemed happy to meet a woman nearer her own age.

"Mum must often be so lonely," Maramy thought sadly.

Kristina was dressed smartly in a dark blue velvet suit, with a light blue ruffled blouse. Her court shoes, also dark blue, were high-heeled and embellished with a sparkling buckle in front. Her little handbag was a matching blue. "Where did she get the exact shades for her bag and shoes?" Maramy wondered. Kristina's golden hair piled high on a perfect forehead was a startling contrast to Maramy's own blue-black curly hair.

Though Maramy had worn her best evening suit, of which she did not have many, she felt she did not look half as smart as her new friend. She also had a simpler, meeker personality. Her black suit was set off by a while blouse and white court shoes. Her handbag was also white. Maramy had always liked the combination of black and white. She wore dangling black earrings of an intricate design. She had always loved and tried to collect specially designed earrings that were unusual and distinctive. Her make-up was light and natural, hardly noticeable. She was a very elegant and beautiful young woman in her own self-effacing way.

"Be careful not to be too late," her mother warned.

"No complaints?" Maramy thought to herself. Her mother had taken her daughter's evening out much better than Maramy had expected. "Bye, mum," she addressed her mother, kissing her on the forehead, and wishing Kristina's aunt goodbye. She had shown her the tiny kitchen where she would find the brand of tea her mother loved, and the bought currant cake, together with a packet of ginger biscuits that both Maramy and her mother always enjoyed.

Kristina said to her aunt, "Veronica, thanks so much. We'll try not to be too late." The girls left the house and wended their way to the car, a little sedan that somehow suited Kristina's personality.

Kristina was an agile driver. Her reflexes were quick and she had her wits about her. "This restaurant is said to be in a very beautiful indoor garden. The food, it is told, is superb and not expensive. Maybe we should have planned to go to a pub with the hope of meeting some nice guys, but we could always do that another time. For now, I'm just hungry and longing for a good and tasty meal," Kristina explained.

"It's o.k. by me," Maramy answered. "I'm not looking for any guys. Just sitting at dinner and talking is fine with me."

CHAPTER 6

Quite soon Kristina veered off into a little side-lane. A strong smell of roses reached their nostrils. The foliage was luscious, and graceful palm-trees paved the lane. Kristina parked the car, and they stepped out. Facing them was a large courtyard with wooden tables covered with stark white tablecloths, and six very solid wooden chairs at each table.

On both sides of the courtyard were exquisite gardens, with mostly roses of all different shapes, sizes and colours. Roses had always been Maramy's favorite flower. One large bush had roses that were almost velvet black in colour. Maramy's passion was vivid red roses, and here they were in abundance, petals unfolding in all their beauty. There were also white roses and yellow, pink and deeper pink, all creating the most vibrant display Maramy had ever encountered.

Dazzled by the beauty around them, they hardly noticed the smartly uniformed young waiter at their side. "Where would you like to be seated?" he asked courteously.

"Do you have a table for two?" Kristina queried.

"Yes, only it is in the corner, over there," the waiter replied, pointing to a little table by a large white gate leading to the pathway towards the garden.

"That will do, thank you," said Kristina politely. He led the way, and pulled their chairs away for them to be seated. He returned with a silver-embossed menu. "Take your time," he said, "I'll be back to take your order."

"What a really beautiful place this is," Kristina gushed.

Maramy's attention was suddenly elsewhere. Two men were standing by the gate. One was older, handsome and well-built, with silvery hair at his temples. The other, younger man was tall, strikingly handsome and extremely dynamic. Maramy's eyes were drawn to him like a magnet, and at that instant he glanced her way. Their eyes locked, and Maramy felt her stomach churn. "Oh, Lord," she thought, "Could this be love at first sight?"

She tore her eyes away from him. Kristina was looking at her quizzically. "He's ever so handsome," she said. "You seem to be completely smitten."

Maramy tried to laugh it off, but she could not understand her feelings at that moment. It was as though the whole world had turned upside down.

CHAPTER 7

The waiter returned, and they ordered their meal. The menu was simple. When their plates were brought to them on a silver tray, they both gasped in surprise. The meal was abundant, beautifully and artistically served, and beside each plate was a perfectly formed red rose. The meat was done to perfection and the salads were perfectly blended and tastefully arranged on separate plates. The potatoes were golden-brown, and crusty rolls lay in a beautiful rattan basket. Even the drinking glasses were of sparkling cut glass, shining like crystal in the light of the low chandelier above them.

Kristina busied herself eating heartily, and Maramy took the opportunity to glance at the young man again. She found his gaze fixed upon her, a somewhat shocked look on his face. "Could he have felt the impact too?" she wondered.

Maramy had had no experience at all with men. Her brother had seen to that, also blocking her wish to do compulsory army service. He had made the excuse of their ailing mother to get her a release. She had remained an inexperienced, innocent virgin, invariably shocked at the careless talk of some of the girls at the office, who gloated with relish about their affairs.

Maramy found herself blushing, and hurriedly began to eat her meal. She and Kristina made small talk. Kristina told her about her past life in Russia, and the difficulties she had had coming to Israel and starting a new life. "My father was a stern, harsh man," she told Maramy. "He showed no love, and was always critical. My mother was a darling, and we were always close. When she died two years ago I could not bear to go on living. My Aunt Veronica is my mother's sister. She never married and she loves me with a fierce, protecting love. When she saw my suffering, and the fact that I could not get on with my father who had lost no time in taking a new wife, she arranged that we both come away to Israel.

"Change place, change luck," she always said. 'It was very hard at first, but we managed to find work, and my aunt has some money that was bequeathed to her by a woman for whom she had been a caregiver for some years. We have a small apartment; we both drive, and manage to get by."

"I bought the car with loans as a new immigrant, and it has become indispensable to us. My aunt is wonderful to me, except that she keeps hoping I'll marry a millionaire some day."

"With your looks and personality you just might," said Maramy encouragingly. She had seen heads turn when they walked in. Kristina would make an impression anywhere.

Kristina and Maramy ate gingerly, relishing every morsel. From the corner of her eye Maramy kept glancing at the handsome young man she had so vividly noticed before. Now he was seated at a table nearby. Each time she looked his way, their glances locked. It seemed they could hardly keep their eyes off each other.

The two girls ordered dessert and coffee. The pastries were a work of art, the famous Arab sweets beautifully served on a gleaming silver platter. The coffee, steaming and aromatic, with the delicious taste of cardamom, was stimulating and refreshing.

Kristina insisted on paying the bill, saying, "You can pay next time."

When they stood up to leave, the young man quickly arose from his table and came towards them. "Did you enjoy the meal?" he asked solicitously.

"Very, very much. Everything was perfect," they reassured him.

"We also enjoyed the lovely well-tended garden," Maramy added.

"Yes," he said. "I see to it that it is well looked after. My father owns this restaurant, and I'm the manager. I'm an engineer by profession, but I enjoy this work, especially in the evenings when the place is full."

"We'll come again," Kristina assured him.

"Please do," he replied. I'll be happy to see you. By the way, my name is Ahmed."

They wished him good-bye and walked to the car. "Can you believe it? He's an Arab. An Arab with light brown hair and blue eyes!" Maramy expostulated. Maramy's heart had sunk as soon as she heard his name. She was deeply disappointed.

CHAPTER 8

Back home, they said their goodbyes and Maramy thanked Veronica warmly. She was surprised when her mother embraced Veronica and said sweetly, "I so enjoyed your company. Do come again." Veronica promised she would, and waving gaily, Kristina and Veronica drove off into the night.

Maramy was restless all night. She kept seeing the piercing blue eyes so intent on her. "An Arab," she kept saying to herself. "An Arab! I won't be seeing him again anyway," she comforted herself, but this thought backfired as she was already filled with longing to see him again. His deep but musical voice had thrilled her to the core and carried her away to a heavenly world she had never experienced before, till the sound of his name had jolted her so abruptly back to reality.

Kristina and Maramy became really close over time, their friendship developing into something very special. Maramy was happy in Kristina's company. She was so outgoing, an extrovert, compared to the retiring Maramy. They met a few times after work, but did not return to the restaurant of their first outing.

One bright summer morning Maramy was waiting for the bus to take her to work, when suddenly a large silver car stopped beside her. She recognized the handsome Arab of her dreams, Ahmed. He beckoned her to enter, and as she seated herself comfortably beside him, he asked." Where can I drop you?"

"I'm on my way to work," she replied, and explained to him the location of her work. "I hope it is not out of your way," she said.

Ahmed answered laughingly, "And what if it is? I'm in no hurry to go anywhere. I have time on my hands, I'll leave you right at your place of work."

"Thanks," she said shortly, all the while fighting the pounding of her heart and the churning of her stomach.

She realised that what she felt for Ahmed was more than a passing attraction. "Oh, no!" she thought to herself, remembering the long nights her thoughts had been only of him. "I've fallen in love with him. This is love. This feeling of joy at being by his side."

He also seemed thoughtful and pensive. As they neared the building she worked in, he asked her gently, "Can I give you a lift tomorrow also?"

A surge of happiness filled her being. "If it is not too much trouble for you," she answered.

"Okay, I'll pick you up at the bus stop at the same time."

She thanked him as she stepped out of the car, and walked briskly towards the lift. "Shall I tell Kristina?" she wondered. "Yes, she is my good friend and I cannot be deceptive with her. I will tell her today."

When Kristina heard that Maramy had arrived at work in Ahmed's car, she was thrilled and happy for her friend. Kristina, with her sexy figure and lovely face, had many admirers. Maramy, no less beautiful, was, however, not conspicuous in her dark and quiet beauty. "You must continue to see him," Kristina advised her friend.

"But he's an Arab," Maramy stated sadly.

"So what if he is?" Kristina asked. See if he is a decent human being. That's what counts. Give yourself a chance. If you find that he is not nice or has unforgivable faults, don't continue. But if he is decent and you like him, there is no reason to stop seeing him. You'll only know by getting to know him better."

"Oh, Kristina," Maramy marveled to herself. "You are so good, and for you life is so simple. No worries about race or discrimination. Wish there were more like you around."

For Ahmed and Kristina it became a morning ritual. He was almost always there before her, and though he did not speak too much while driving, they did manage to get to know each other and found themselves completely compatible. She learnt that he an Arab, but not overly devout. She in turn explained to him that her mother was very traditional and kept the Sabbath and the dietary laws and other observances of the Jewish faith. "I, myself, judge a person by his goodness and kindness and not by what religion he belongs to," Maramy explained, and Ahmed agreed.

CHAPTER 9

One night, events took a surprising turn for Maramy. Arriving home a little earlier than usual from her date with Ahmed, she noticed her mother and Veronica sitting close together, looking down at a page in a photo album. She heard her mother explain to Veronica, "My husband was a brave and wonderful man. He never shirked his duty. When asked if he was willing to be a part of a group travelling to Iraq to smuggle arms to Israel, he immediately took up the challenge. It turned out to be a horrendous experience for him. In the photograph you can see him with his young commanding officer, Lieutenant Ellis of the British Forces."

"Ellis was brave and risked his life, but the plot was discovered and Ellis was shot before my husband's eyes.

His girlfriend, Pnina, who had also participated in the assignment, was grief-stricken and broken-hearted.

"My husband never got over the incident. He made me promise never to tell the children, who were then very young, as he wanted them to look on him as a father, not a hero. But he *was* a hero, and he was always my hero. He took part in other dangerous assignments after that, but the incident when his beloved commander of the mission was shot before his eyes was one he would never recover from."

Maramy kept away till her mother had finished narrating her story. She recollected the photograph of her father with a young, dashing-looking man in uniform. She had always been fascinated by the photograph of the impressive young soldier with the sensitive face and determined look. Once she had asked her father, "Who is this handsome young man beside you in the photograph?"

Her father had answered nonchalantly, "Just a passing friend from the old days when I was quite young."

Maramy quickly decided she would pretend she had not overheard the story. She waited silently, and stepped into the room only after a few minutes had elapsed. On her entering the room, her mother hurriedly put the album away and asked Maramy how come she had arrived earlier than usual. Maramy explained that she had a slight headache and wanted to get to bed early.

Maramy was stunned by the story she had just heard for the first time, and her heart ached for the young soldier who had so tragically lost his life for his beliefs. "His poor girl-friend. Wonder what happened to her eventually?" Maramy wondered. "Thank G-d my father and the others escaped. I am lucky to have been the daughter of such a wonderful man."

Veronica warmly took leave of Maramy and her mother. Maramy knew her mother was absolutely not in favour of her daughter's nights out, but her annoyance was softened by Veronica's presence. They seemed to have become good friends.

Maramy kissed her mother's cheek, saying, "Goodnight, mum. Sweet dreams!" and hurried off to prepare for bed before any tirade began and the usual complaints of her mother would not be heard by her.

As she lay in bed, she wondered if this was the reason her mother had nagged her father to leave the kibbutz. She had probably been afraid of his being called to risk his life again. She could not sleep for hours, her mind churning over the surprising story she had heard that evening. When she did fall asleep, it was a troubled one, with dreams of the handsome young soldier, her rugged-looking father and the danger they had shared that had ended so tragically for one of them. "Young men risking their lives for their ideals. Is it ever worth it?" she asked herself.

In spite of her bad night's rest she woke up early, and a new day had begun.

CHAPTER 10

Maramy knew her problem was not an easy one to solve. "I must approach Ahmed with the subject of our difference of religion," she decided.

After a few months of meetings and no talk of their future together, Maramy realised it was time to discuss the situation openly. Their next meeting was to be a decisive one.

Maramy dressed carefully, and knew she was looking her best. Her hair and eyes shone, her skin was glowing, her figure trim and feminine. Ahmed's eyes shone with pleasure and admiration when they met. They sat in their usual dark corner at his restaurant, locking hands across the table. Ahmed seemed in a pensive mood, hesitant and deep in thought. Over a cup of her favorite cardamom flavored Turkish coffee, Maramy plunged bravely into her well-rehearsed speech about their future together.

"You are an Arab, I am Jewish. Is it possible to have a happy life together?" she asked.

He did not answer for some time. Then he gave her his shocking reply, "I've been thinking of this for a long time. We can never marry, but we can live together. There is no other way."

Maramy thought she had not heard correctly. "Never marry? Live together?" she repeated in a daze. "What? You want me to be your kept woman, to never have a family, to never have the experience of giving birth? Your life can go on as usual, but mine has to be shattered?"

He heard her in silence, then repeated, "There is no other way."

Maramy dug her nails deeply into the palms of her hands. Was this the honest, righteous man she loved? The one who spoke against suicide bombers and terrorists, who spoke about world peace and the unity of the human race? She stood up, shaking. "Good-bye, Ahmed," she said quietly, and ran out of the restaurant.

The restaurant was located in a secluded area, but she spotted a taxi and hailed it quickly. Ahmed had run towards her, but evidently did not go too far, because as she seated herself in the depths of the taxi and gave instructions for her destination, there was no sign of Ahmed nearby.

Crying bitterly, she reached home, broken-hearted and shattered. "My life has ended," she told herself.

Veronica was with her mum, and they were both surprised to see her home so early. Maramy had to be deceptive again. "Kristina had a headache so we broke it up early," she lied. Her mother always concluded that Maramy went out with Kristina, and Maramy had to continue her deception. Her mother would have had a fit if she knew Maramy had a date with a man, let alone an Arab.

Veronica looked at her sharply, noticing the red eyes and weary gait. "No need to ask questions," she told herself. "Kristina will tell me everything." She picked up her handbag and said good-bye, kissing Maramy's mother on the cheek, and assuring her that she would visit her again soon.

Maramy made her mother's bedtime chocolate drink, kissed her good night, and hurried to her room. Her bitter tears fell fast and strong. She felt physically and mentally ill. She did not sleep a wink all night.

CHAPTER 11

The next morning, Maramy did not go to work. She felt too ill. Her mother, for once, showed some concern. Maramy never took time off from work. Kristina came to see her straight after work. They went into Maramy's room, and Maramy, sobbing bitterly, told her good friend the whole story. "What would I do without Kristina? I am so thankful to have such a good friend," thought Maramy.

Kristina held her hand, soothing her with loving words. "It will be okay. It will be okay," she kept repeating. She herself was not in the best of moods. She'd had a few heartaches lately too. Her last boyfriend, a Russian immigrant like herself, had a real drinking problem. Also, he had disclosed that he had applied for a Canadian immigrant visa, and was hoping to leave for Canada as soon as possible.

Her own problems were pushed into the background now, as she gave her friend sympathy and love, if not much hope. She had worried about the relationship between Ahmed and Maramy, knowing that Maramy's mum was bigoted, and that marrying an Arab would be a calamity for Maramy. However, she had never disclosed her doubts to Maramy, and the thought had never struck her that Ahmed would not want to marry her beautiful friend. She left Maramy with a heavy heart, full of sympathy for her friend's pain.

Maramy decided she would take a much earlier bus from that point on, in order to avoid seeing Ahmed. Though heartsick and numb, she continued her daily routine as usual.

In the days to come, Ahmed did not try to see her, and she knew the affair was over. "So be it," she thought to herself. "It was not to be. I have to forge my life ahead, and forget about love or being loved."

Maramy fell into a deep depression. Kristina, the ever-faithful friend, tried her best to cheer her up. "Come on, Maramy, you're beautiful, you're clever, you can shine out in life."

Nothing seemed to help. Maramy threw herself into work at the office with a determination and energy bordering on frenzy. She ate very little, and lost a great deal of weight. There were dark circles under her eyes. Kristina was worried about her friend, but felt helpless in the face of Maramy's misery.

She herself should have been extremely happy. At last she had met the man of her dreams, handsome, kind and courteous. Also rich! What more could she ask for? However, her happiness was marred by Maramy's continuing depression. Kristina felt frustrated. "How can I help Maramy if Maramy will not help herself?" she pondered.

Maramy's mother, as usual, was indifferent to her daughter's plight. Her plaintive voice was often heard in complaint. She was upset that Veronica did not come to see her as often as before, and wondered why Maramy did not go out. Veronica had usually come to keep her company when Maramy was out, supposedly with Kristina.

Kristina tried her best to take Maramy out as before, but Maramy seemed listless and not in the mood. However,

Kristina managed to get a promise from Maramy that she would start going out with her again. She had not yet told Maramy of her present happiness with her new boyfriend, partly because of Maramy's unhappiness, and partly because she knew Maramy would not be a third in the company of two lovebirds. However, she was willing to meet Maramy alone whenever her friend was ready to go out again.

CHAPTER 12

When Maramy's brother made one of his rare visits, he was shocked at his sister's appearance. He was also blunt and cruel about it. "Maramy, you look awful. What man would look at you? You look half-starved, almost ugly. What on earth is wrong with you? You had better see a doctor. There is definitely something wrong with you."

His harsh words had some effect on Maramy. "*I have to get over this pain,*" she decided. She forced herself to eat more, started meeting Kristina after work, and she cried less at night. The pain did not go away, but it lost its sharp edge just a little bit.

Her brother brought an older, charming man over one evening. He seemed interested in Maramy. Her brother encouraged the courtship in every way he could.

His friend with the ubiquitous name of Joe was well-established in life. He had a Mercedes, the latest model, lived in a large and beautiful villa, and was generous. He brought expensive gifts to Maramy's mother, who was completely charmed by him.

The only one who disliked him on sight was Kristina. "He's not what he seems," she told Maramy. She did not tell Maramy that his glances were lascivious, and that her mistrust was built not only on intuition, but also on those sly, sideways glances that he threw at her from time to time. She avoided being around him, telling Maramy that she was busy with her own boyfriend, who did really want to see her as much as possible. He adored Kristina and his adoration brought a glow of happiness to her face, enhancing her beauty.

Maramy's brother. Ofer, kept pushing Joe on to her at every opportunity. The fact that Joe was much older than his sister did not bother him. In fact, he saw it as an advantage for her. Being older, he would be more understanding and caring than a younger man. Maramy was now twenty-two. She would have to marry some day.

Joe had money, and that was the most deciding factor for Ofer. "They'll get off my back if they have his money," Ofer thought selfishly. The fact that it was his mother who always begged from him did not matter. He lumped them both together, and though Maramy had never asked him for money or anything else, he thought his responsibility to her would end if she married well.

"How long can I stand up against my brother and mother?" Maramy wondered. Joe brought her expensive gifts and took her to the best nightclubs and restaurants. He always seemed kind and considerate. Gradually Maramy came to think of him as an escape from her misery. "But I don't love him," she thought sadly. "There are times when he even repels me, I don't know why."

Joe's visits became more frequent, and his attentions more forceful. Plus, Maramy's brother would not leave her alone, insisting at every opportunity that she agree to marry Joe. His threats were frightening. "You'll be an old maid with no one to care for you," he would tell her. "Take your chance while you have it."

"Ahmed," her heart cried, "why can't you return to me? Why can't you feel the same as I do? Why can't I forget you? When will this ache in my heart pass away? Will it ever?"

One day, Maramy was more depressed than ever. The firm she had worked so hard for, had had to close down due to an economic crisis, and she was left jobless. Her savings were dwindling, and her mother's demands were stronger than ever. She did not see as much of Kristina as before, presumably because Kristina was busy dating her new boyfriend. Maramy was happy for Kristina. She deserved the best. All the while, Joe visited often, with his ready charm and offerings of love.

CHAPTER 13

Tired of being sad and lonely, Maramy finally gave in. She phoned Kristina, saying sadly, "Kristina, there is nothing left for me. I have no choice."

Kristina cried "Oh, Maramy, I wish I could help you! I just don't know how I can. I feel you are making a mistake. Maybe you will find another job soon. Maybe things will work out without you taking this drastic step. You don't love Joe, and even though you will not have money worries, I hope you will not have worries of any other kind."

Maramy, hot tears pouring down her face, cried in utter despair, "I do not see any other way out. I have not been able to find a job for the past three months. I am afraid of leaving mother alone during the intifada. Every time there is another incident, she gets hysterical.

She is so fragile and nervous. In any case, with so much unemployment, I won't have much of a chance."

"What about your rich brother?" Kristina asked sarcastically. She had never liked him, seeing him for what he was — a pompous, selfish tyrant.

"Oh, no help from there. He is trying to force my hand to marry Joe. Besides, he is too engrossed in his own affairs, his wife and children, to care much about us. You know what a hard nut his wife is. She is the one who holds the purse-strings, and the only one he is afraid of," Maramy told Kristina.

"Two awful monsters," Kristina thought. "If only Maramy were stronger in character and could hold them in check and not let them bully her."

Joe seemed overjoyed when Maramy finally consented to marry him. They were in a high-class restaurant where, as usual, he had ordered lavishly. Over a glass of expensive wine he had again proposed to her. When she agreed, he could hardly believe that she had consented. He wanted her for her beauty and fine brain. She would be an asset to him. On the other hand, he felt her lack of enthusiasm. It bothered his ego, but he knew that he always got what he went after, sooner or later.

Maramy's mother's usual selfish reaction was, 'Who will look after me? Who will cook my meals, clean the house, pay the bills?"

Maramy's brother quelled her fears. "I will help you," he promised, and continued, "also, Maramy will be marrying a wealthy man. She will be able to provide you with every comfort." As usual, her brother Ofer fixed the main responsibility on Maramy, not himself. He had taken good care of his own money for the past few years, making Maramy pay all she could spare toward the upkeep of the house and their mother's extravagant demands

"My heart cries for you, Ahmed!" she silently told herself many times a day. "Why could you not feel the same for me as I feel for you? I was prepared to face the world with the thought of your love for me giving me courage to go on. Now I am lost! I am lost!"

CHAPTER 14

Kristina's support was Maramy's only strength now. Kristina was completely against her decision to marry Joe. Every fiber of her being knew it was a mistake, but she also realized she had to support Maramy. The poor girl felt there was no alternative but to survive by sacrificing her ideals, her hopes, and her heart. Kristina, happy in her own love, still felt deeply for her friend and her pain and unhappiness.

Kristina, an angel among humans, was deeply concerned by her friend's plight. She wondered, "Should I find Ahmed and warn him of Maramy's fate? Will it help?" In the end she decided not to interfere. It was not her place to do so.

Meantime the new love of her life, Ferdie, listened patiently to Kristina's worries about her friend. He was so proud of her, for with her outstanding beauty, she also had a heart of gold. He loved her so much. Unlike her former boyfriend, he was serious and sober.

They had met at her place of work. He was a computer engineer recently promoted to a higher post. He was kind and gentle, and Kristina in turn loved him and appreciated the qualities that her former boyfriend had lacked. Maybe he was not outstandingly handsome, but he was a good man who would always put her needs before his own. She felt serene and contented in her love.

It had been hard to make her former boyfriend understand that their affair was finished. She had a sense of peace and relief that she had been saved from great unhappiness, and she blessed the day that Ferdie had entered her life and shown her a way of loving that had kindness, understanding and respect, not just passion and a tempestuous relationship that brought only pain. If only her dear friend Maramy would have had the same luck.

Joe was generous in his gifts and attention to Maramy. He took her to expensive restaurants. He even bought Maramy's mother gold ornaments, trinkets and items of clothing, such as embroidered kaftans and nightdresses of the purest silk. He won Maramy's mother over completely. She was gushing and effusive in her praise of him, and was now sure that her daughter had made the right choice.

Joe brought Maramy home in his bright, flashy car, "Good evening, mum," he told her mother. He handed her a big gold box of the best Belgian chocolates. Her mother was over the moon. She loved chocolates almost as much as the bracelets and chains he often brought her.

"Thank you, son," she gushed. Her own son had never bothered to bring her any present, except once on a High Holiday.

One evening Joe came unexpectedly early, and seemed to be in an unusually bright mood. He kissed Maramy's mother, and imperiously told Maramy, "Maramy, let's go. I have reserved a table at the Grand Beach."

Maramy went in for a quick shower, and dressed in her favorite blue silk. She dreaded the evening ahead of her. She could not bear his hands on her. The only way she found to not show her dislike was by pretending it was Ahmed who was embracing her.

Joe was not always pleasant, and she often saw a side to his nature that he tried hard to hide. He often found fault with the service at restaurants and made fun of others - their clothes, their voices, their way of walking, their weight, height, etc. He was not kind, and seemed to look for faults in others. To Maramy, though, he was always attentive and never failed to pay her compliments at every opportunity. Her beauty pleased him, and as heads turned to look at her, he was proud and possessive, and pleased that she was his.

CHAPTER 15

This evening was to be special. Joe ordered the main course, a delicious concoction of juicy prunes and tender meat. Maramy once again felt faint resentment at his self-assuredness in never consulting her on his choice of the menu.

After ordering, Joe said, "Maramy, I want to fix the date of our wedding. I want to marry you as soon as possible."

Now her heart fell. "How can I postpone this?" she wondered.

Joe went on, "I want us to get married on the 5th of June. Is that okay with you?"

As usual, he had fixed the date and she had no say. "It's too soon," she remonstrated. "I can never be ready in such a short time."

"Nonsense!" he answered. "I will give you the money for your bridal clothing, and I will fix the time and place, the menu, the guest list, etc. You don't have to worry your pretty little head about anything."

Maramy was despondent, but tried not to show him any sign of her heavy heart. Her fate was sealed. She was to get married to a man she did not love, someone she often did not even like.

That night she cried herself to sleep. "Ahmed, Ahmed, I must forget you!" she said sadly to herself. She was afraid of what lay before her, a grand wedding, and then what? Ahmed's rejection had hurt her badly. She had been so sure that he loved her just as she loved him. Now she had to put that in the past and go on with the future.

Maramy, with Kristina's help, chose her wedding gown, veil, and shoes. She also bought several outfits she felt she would need later. Kristina felt her friend's helplessness and melancholy, but there was not much she could do now, except hope for the best. She did try tentatively to dissuade her friend from marrying Joe, but realised that Maramy had made up her mind, though reluctantly, and there was no turning back.

Kristina and her aunt, Veronica, also took Maramy's mother shopping, and bought her a beautiful outfit for the wedding. Kristina's mother's eyes gleamed with excitement. Her future son-in-law was nothing if not generous, and she anticipated many comfortable years ahead for her after Maramy's marriage. Even her son, Ofer, was in a good mood these days, praising Maramy's decision, and telling her how much he and his wife and children were looking forward to the wedding.

"Yes," thought Kristina when she heard his exuberance about the matter. "You and your wife and children will have the opportunity to show off, and to enjoy yourselves without spending much from your own pocket." The more she saw of Joe the more she disliked him, and tried to avoid meeting him whenever she could. When possible, she kept her fiancé at her side if she knew she would be seeing Joe.

CHAPTER 16

The days passed too quickly for Maramy, and before she knew it her wedding day had arrived. What a wedding! The hall was filled with beautiful flowers. Maramy noticed that her favourite, red roses, were not much to be seen amongst the other glowing colors. Joe had not noticed that red roses were her favourite flowers. There was much he did not take the care to notice or remember. Even the music was to his taste, not hers. She resented this, but knew she did not have the guts to reprimand Joe about his lack of feeling for her wishes and taste. His was so much the stronger personality, and she wilted before him.

The hall was the most expensive and well-known available. After the rabbi pronounced them man and wife and after Joe had performed the traditional custom of breaking the glass with his foot, there was much clapping, shaking of hands, and congratulations all round. Ofer and his wife came to the dais and wished Maramy happiness, taking the opportunity of telling her she had made the right choice.

"Am I the only lucky one?" Maramy thought. "Is Joe not lucky to marry me? Am I not worth anything?"

Maramy looked ravishing in a lace long-sleeved dress studded with pearls. Her lovely hair shone against the whiteness of the delicate veil. Her mother was tastefully dressed in the expensive suit paid for by her future son-in-law. Her eyes gleamed as she envisaged the luxury she and her daughter would now enjoy. She was an innately selfish woman, and did not give a thought to her daughter's happiness. In her eyes Maramy was making a good match to a rich and successful man who would keep them both in comfort. Besides, Joe had been very good to her, buying her expensive presents, often including her in their dinner dates, and flattering her at every opportunity. Yes, he was a good catch for her daughter.

Veronica was beside her, looking smart and distinguished in a new, beautifully-cut dress, her hair and make-up perfect. She looked much younger than her years. However, she also was not happy for Maramy, and worried about the girl's future.

Kristina was stunning in a gold-spangled, fitted dress showing to perfection her beautiful figure. She was the chief bridesmaid and made a magnificent impression. Her fiancé could not take his eyes off her, showing clearly the adoration and love he felt.

Kristina thoughtfully held Maramy's hand for a moment, pressing her palm gently, and whispering, "Don't worry, Maramy, everything will be all right." In her heart she felt only pain for her friend. She believed Joe was a fake. She was sure of one thing - Maramy deserved better.

CHAPTER 17

The wedding night was a disaster. Maramy was shy and reticent, and Joe was impatient. He showed no tenderness. He now possessed a valuable prize — a beautiful and intelligent wife. His friends would envy him. He had riches, success, and now a beautiful young bride.

He had drunk too much, and Maramy felt nauseous. Well, she had burned her bridges behind her, and now had no alternative but to grin and bear it.

Joe was generous, and they lived in luxury. Their home was a mansion, spacious and well-kept. She did not need to do housework, as they had maids and a cook. However, Joe was out often and she felt deeply lonely. Joe had not wanted her to work.

Kristina was busy with work and with the love of her life, and was now planning her own wedding. However, she never failed to phone Maramy often, and tried to meet her as much as possible, mostly in restaurants and cafes. She avoided Maramy's home for fear of being around Joe, whom she continued to dislike, perhaps more than ever now, as she sensed her friend's loneliness and sadness.

Maramy's mother was ensconced in a new apartment on the other side of town. She had a maid to see to all her wants, and a loyal caregiver who did not answer back, complain or show impatience. Joe had seen to it that she would be happy and well taken care of, but stood his ground and said that she would not stay with them in the same house.

Ofer visited her sometimes, and was glad to see his mother well taken care of, which took any pressure off him. He also visited Joe and Maramy from time to time, but practically ignored Maramy, spending the time drinking with Joe and enjoying the good liquor provided.

"What a pain in the neck Ofer is," Kristina often thought. "He doesn't care a bit about his sister's happiness. He is selfish like his mother."

Maramy's sorrow grew greater every day. Her husband had soon become indifferent to her. She was pregnant, sick most of the time, and felt very much alone. "If it were not for Kristina I would go mad," she often thought.

Faithful friend that she was, Kristina made it a point to see Maramy whenever she could, in spite of her own busy life and her happiness with her fiancé. She felt the resentment Joe had for her whenever he happened to be present. It did not bother her too much. She disliked him and pitied Maramy.

Maramy's mother almost never visited her daughter, expecting Maramy to come to her instead. The only times she visited was with Veronica, who brought her in her car. Veronica was a good woman, always helpful and kind. She was planning a visit to her sister in Russia, but shelved her plans for the time being in order to be with Kristina for her wedding.

One twilight evening Kristina and her boyfriend came over and insisted on taking Maramy out. Now in her ninth month, it was hard for Maramy to move much. However, they took her in their car to a fancy restaurant. The evening was particularly enjoyable. Kristina and Ferdie talked of their impending wedding, giving Maramy details of their arrangements. They also talked of the baby soon to arrive, saying she would be beautiful like Maramy.

Maramy was surprised that they were so sure it would be a girl. Her husband, Joe, counted on it being a boy. More relaxed than she had been for ages, Maramy returned home in a more hopeful spirit. "Maybe the baby will change Joe for the better. Maybe he will stay at home more often, and drink less."

CHAPTER 18

Wakened suddenly from her optimistic reverie, Maramy felt a heavy hand slap her face. "Where have you been, you slut?" Joe asked angrily.

She could not answer, as she was in shock. Joe was often verbally abusive, but had never raised his hand to her before. Another heavy blow descended on her delicate face, and she felt intense pain. "I was with Kristina," she managed to say as she rushed through the door and locked herself in the bathroom. His slurred words followed her, as he banged angrily on the door. Terrified, she did not dare open the door. She sat in the bathroom the whole night, trembling.

In the morning she heard the sound of Joe's car. The maid was on leave and she was alone. When she heard the car leave, she felt it was safe to come out. She made sure Joe was not around, and then quickly phoned Kristina.

Kristina left work as early as she could, and came quickly to Maramy's home. However, the house was locked from the outside, and she realised that Joe had locked Maramy in. Kristina spoke to Maramy through the door. "Leave him," she said. "He is a monster. He is destroying you!"

"He'll follow me and kill me if I try to leave," answered Maramy tremulously. It was obvious that she was frightened.

"Shall I go to the police?" Kristina asked.

"No! No, please don't do that," Maramy pleaded.

After comforting Maramy as best she could, Kristina left, her heart heavy. What could she do to help her friend?

That night the baby was born. Joe had returned home sober and when he saw she needed his help, he rose to the occasion. After all, he wanted a son! He rushed her to the hospital, in anticipation of the son he was sure he would be blessed with. He had not apologized to Maramy for the night before, even though he noticed the fiery marks on her cheek and the swelling on her face. He just was not the type to admit to his faults or face them.

Maramy suffered many hours of agony during labor. The nurses asked her about the swelling and welts on her face, but she lied that she had hurt herself. They wondered if that was the truth, but her husband seemed so pleasant and charming that they could not believe that he would do this to his pregnant wife.

The baby, an extraordinarily beautiful girl with clear features, was a balm to her mother's aching heart. When Joe came to visit later — he had not stayed with her during her ordeal — he did not bother to hide his disappointment at having a daughter instead of the son he so wished for. He did not bring her flowers or an apology for the night before.

Kristina came rushing in when she heard the news. Her face beaming, she handed Maramy many gifts for her and the baby. Veronica also visited, her arms full of beautiful bouquets for the new mother. Kristina put the red roses in water in the big, clumsy hospital vase, arranging them carefully.

"Thank you, G-d, for such a friend!" Maramy thought for the umpteenth time. "What would I do without Kristina?"

Neither her brother, his wife, nor her mother visited her in hospital. She was sad, but felt she now had her beautiful baby daughter to comfort her. She felt sorry for her mother, who loved Ofer's sons, even though they did not give her the time of the day. She wasn't too well these days, and had declined Veronica's offer to drive her to the hospital.

Kristina came as often as she could, mostly accompanied by her fiancé, Ferdie, who one could see clearly was besotted with Kristina. His love shone from his soft brown eyes as he looked at her. It was cheering to see them together.

Kristina was devoted to the baby. She was thrilled to hold the child in her arms. She was a great help to Maramy whenever she was able to come and visit. Maramy noticed that Kristina seemed to avoid Joe, and she mostly came with her fiancé. Joe on the other hand, seemed hostile to their visits.

Joe did not seem to care much about the baby. The only objection he had was that the baby should not be called Kristina, as Maramy wished to do. So Maramy had no other choice but to give another name to her daughter. Joe wanted the child named after his mother, though he had once mentioned that he had never been close to her. Maramy's mother hinted that she would like the child to bear her name but Maramy did not want this as she was also not very close to her mother, and did not like the name Arabella. What would she name the child? In the end she decided on the name Carina, mentioning to Kristina that it was nearest to her name. Kristina understood that Joe would not want the baby named after her. She told Maramy that Carina was a lovely name, and hugged and kissed both mother and child.

CHAPTER 19

Joe became more and more violent, drank a lot, and was hardly at home. Meantime, Kristina's fiancé told Maramy that Joe had made advances to Kristina. Maramy was not surprised. She had guessed this quite some time ago.

One day Joe came in raging. He beat her up, screaming, "I'll kill you." Maramy was terrified. The baby was sleeping in her crib. Maramy was afraid to let Joe know she was expecting another child. "Why are you angry?" she asked timidly. "Shut up," he yelled, "you're living on my money, shut up." He was drunk. "What will happen to us?" Maramy thought fearfully. He had beaten her before for no reason and she had got used to his cruel moods.

He loved good food and drink, and as the years went by, he had become bloated and was gradually losing his good looks. He seemed aware of this and it made him angry. He resented Maramy's beauty and became more and more suspicious. He was indifferent to the child and Maramy feared for her. When Joe heard that Maramy was pregnant again, he showed no tenderness, and his heavy, intoxicated breath disgusted her.

One day she called her faithful friend Kristina. "Please accompany me to the doctor?" she pleaded.

The ultrasound showed a boy child, and when Maramy related to Joe, he was, surprisingly, very pleased. "A son," he said, "I've always dreamed of a son."

Maramy was happy to see Joe's reaction. So different from her first pregnancy. He even showed concern for Maramy, which pleased her immensely.

When the baby was born, Joe seemed to be a proud father. He had a party for relatives and friends. Joe did not have any close relatives, so those attending were Maramy's mother, who was still always complaining; her brother, who was grumpy and unemotional; his showy wife (the boys did not come); and Kristina and Ferdie, Maramy's true friends. There were also a group of Joe's drinking buddies, most of them coarse and uncouth.

Maramy was nervous during the circumcision ceremony, but after one long, angry wail, the baby was quiet and soon fell asleep.

Her little daughter, now three years old, was with the maid, but soon left her hand to run up to Kristina, whom she was very fond of.

"You look so beautiful, Maramy," Kristina whispered, kissing her friend. "Please look after yourself. Your pregnancy and childbirth have not been easy. Take care,"

Maramy appreciated her friend's concern, and answered, "I will, Kristina. I have two innocent lives dependent on me now."

The days passed relatively quietly. The children were growing well, but Joe's eyes lit up only for their son. They had named him Justin, after Joe's father. "My poor daughter," Maramy thought. "She must feel so neglected by her father."

Kristina and Ferdie had been living together for some time now, and had decided it was time to marry and start a family of their own. They were planning a big wedding, and Kristina had already told Maramy they wanted her children to be bridesmaid and pageboy. Kristina adored Maramy's children.

Kristina's aunt, Veronica, had delayed her plans to visit her sister in Russia, as she was waiting expectantly for her beloved niece to fix a date and get married. She would not have missed the wedding for all the gold in the world.

The wedding day arrived, and Joe sullenly took Maramy and the children to the large synagogue. Kristina and Ferdie had both wanted to marry in a synagogue. The reception would be in a large adjoining hall that had been lavishly decorated for the occasion.

The children were charming, and Maramy thought Kristina was the most beautiful bride there ever was. Everyone could see the love between the groom and bride. Their eyes were shining with happiness as they took their vows.

After the ritual breaking of the glass with his foot, Ferdie kissed Kristina and everyone clapped. They had many friends, and Ferdie also had many relatives. At the reception, after a short speech by Ferdie's uncle, the dancing began. The music was quite loud, but there was much enjoyment and merriment. The food was ample and delicious. Everything went smoothly and as desired. Many photographs were taken.

Fortunately, Joe behaved himself and did not drink too much, though liquor was plentiful. He gazed at the bride and groom with something close to disdain and anger. Though not so luxurious as his and Maramy's wedding, it was a very enjoyable affair, but not as formal as theirs had been.

Veronica kept close to Maramy's mother throughout the reception. They made an ill-sorted couple, one so bright and positive, the other always grumpy and complaining. Despite their differences, they seemed to have developed a friendship that was strong and caring. Veronica did not want Maramy's mother to be bored or to feel left out, and gave her the attention that her own son and daughter-in-law did not.

All in all, the wedding was one to remember, and everyone went home contented and pleased, except perhaps for Joe, who scowled all the way back home. His son had fallen asleep in his arms. The older child, Carina, was wide-awake and chattered all the way home, to Joe's annoyance. However, he could see that they were both extraordinarily beautiful and bright, and this was a palliative to his angry soul.

CHAPTER 20

Veronica was busy and excited about her impending visit with her sister in Russia. She bought a new suitcase and began carefully packing in preparation. She had willingly postponed her plans because it was important to her to be at Kristina's wedding. Now that it was over, and everything had gone smoothly and well, she was impatient to continue with her travel plans.

Veronica was an impressive woman, who got noticed. She was tall, with a straight back and perfect posture. At first impression, she seemed rather remote and distant, but when one knew her better one was drawn to the warmth of her loving and compassionate nature. She was well loved and respected at work, where she had been given a few promotions, and now held a responsible job that she enjoyed.

She was an attractive woman, with beautiful grey eyes and long lashes, similar to her niece, Kristina. Her hair was warm blonde, and she had taken to dyeing it in the last few years. Her clothes were tailored and well cut, and always perfectly tasteful for the occasion. Her voice was soft and melodious, and her whole bearing was very lady-like and aristocratic.

The bond between Veronica and Kristina was deep. Kristina had once explained to Maramy that she had had such respect and love for her aunt that she had passed her teenage years without causing her any worry or anger. Even Maramy's mother, who never found a good word to say to anyone, had never once been heard to say anything against Veronica. Those who knew Veronica often wondered why she had never married. After all, she must have had plenty of admirers.

One day Kristina confided the reason Veronica was single to Maramy. Years before, even before Kristina was born, Veronica was engaged to a young soldier whom she had loved very much. Before he could return from the front to marry her, he had been killed. The tragedy was so great for Veronica that she could not ever love another man.

Kristina said that Veronica had once shown her a photograph of her fiancé and herself. He was strikingly handsome, and even in the photograph one could see the love they bore each other. Veronica always wore a chain with a locket containing her fiancé's photograph.

Veronica did not know where to park her car while she was away. Both Kristina and Ferdie had cars and there was no place near their apartment where she could keep hers. A colleague at work had told her he had plenty of parking space on the grounds of his large villa, and that she was welcome to park her car there for as long as she wished. He had also told her it would be in safe keeping with him.

Accordingly, she left the car with her friend. She took the bus to her home after declining a lift, as she explained that it was a short way by bus and she had to do some last-minute shopping on the way.

Maramy and Ferdie were to take her to the airport late the next afternoon. Though they insisted on her staying with them for the night, she refused, and told them she would be waiting at home for them to pick her up the next day.

She entered the rather crowded bus, thinking that it had been a long time since she had travelled by bus. It seemed interesting to see so many people on the bus, probably with such varying backgrounds.

There was a shifty-looking man sitting just in front of Veronica. His coat seemed to bulge, and she wondered if she should point him out to the driver or at least change her seat. At that moment, there was a massive explosion and the bus was blown to smithereens. There were people screaming, limbs flying into the air, smoke, fire and pandemonium. A suicide bomber had again done his dirty work, and everyone on the bus was killed and burnt beyond recognition.

CHAPTER 21

The aftermath of Veronica's funeral was overwhelmingly sad. The two friends, Maramy and Kristina, were wrapped in such a heavy mantle of melancholy that neither could function normally. Even Maramy's mother was sad and depressed. She had put up a large photograph of Veronica on her mantelpiece and would just gaze at the picture and sigh. The shock was great and only time would soften the heavy blow they had endured.

Their grief was sharpened by the fact that Veronica had not been able to achieve her dream of visiting Russia and seeing her beloved sister who had been so eagerly awaiting her visit. It seemed such a cruel twist of fate that a wonderful, giving person like Veronica would have had such an untimely death, and have all her dreams shattered by the hate of someone she did not even know.

Quite a few people were killed when the bus blew up, including two young children. The heartache was felt nationwide. However often these brutal attacks occurred, they were always painful and horrific, bringing misery to many families who might never really recover from the loss.

What about those who were severely injured? Was it not almost worse than death to be confined to a wheelchair or hospital bed for life? A friend's young son, a soldier still in his uniform, had been visiting his father's workshop and was badly injured in the same incident of the bus explosion. He was now in a coma in the hospital. Would he ever recover?

Kristina's husband was a rock to the girls in their suffering. His love and devotion would do much in the future to help heal Kristina's pain. He also commiserated with Maramy, whom he knew did not have the comfort of her husband's shoulder to cry on or any kind words from him. To Joe, Veronica was dead and nothing would bring her back, so the incident should be put behind them forever. They had only to look to the future.

He had no patience for the grief of others. He had become more cold and uncaring as time passed. He had patience only for his son, whom he adored. His son, likewise, looked upon him as a hero. There was a bond between the two, to the exclusion of his wife and daughter. Yet the boy equally adored his mother, and was always obedient and loving. He trailed after Carina, who in turn, was extremely attached to her charming young brother.

Maramy worried about the effect Joe's preference for his son would have on Carina, but her daughter went her own blithe way, and was a normal, playful and good little girl. She took no notice of her father's indifference, and was not afraid of him. From a young age she felt it was her duty to protect her mother from her father's taunts and nasty remarks.

"I am so lucky to have such fine children. God bless them," Maramy always told herself. She was also thankful for having the friendship of a wonderful person like Kristina, and also felt blessed for both herself and Kristina that Ferdie was pleased with Kristina's close friendship with Maramy.

Maramy's brother, Ofer, and his wife seldom visited, though Maramy knew that Ofer and Joe often met for drinks. It was as though they felt they had done their duty by attending the graveside and coming during the "shiva" and now there was no need for their presence or for a comforting word to Kristina and Maramy. Especially not to Maramy, for, after all, they felt, she was only a friend and no relation.

Ofer was impatient with his mother if she ever spoke of Veronica, and asked her why she had put her photograph up for all to see. As usual, Maramy's mother never answered him, but did not remove the photograph from its central place in her home. Beneath her crankiness and bitterness, she was an unhappy woman who had lost her beloved husband, and now the only friend she felt she had ever had.

Unfortunately, Maramy's mother did not try to take consolation from her lovely young grandchildren. They were sometimes boisterous, at other times busy with their homework, but she kept away from them and showed her impatience without consideration for their feelings. The children and she seldom met, as she could not travel much now due to ill health. Maramy made it a point to visit her from time to time, but her mother never questioned Maramy about her life or asked if she was content. She also never asked the children about their friends, their school, nor their hobbies.

Poor woman, she did not realize how much she was losing in life by directing her feelings away from her daughter and grandchildren. Strangely, she still ran after Ofer's hulking big sons, who never gave her the time of day or ever bothered to phone her or visit. To her, Ofer and his children could do no wrong. She also continued to kid herself that they cared, probably to avoid the truth that they couldn't care less about her.

CHAPTER 22

Eventually, Kristina and Ferdie decided to move. "I don't want to go too far from you," Kristina told Maramy. They eventually found a bright and spacious apartment not too far from Maramy. Maramy and the children often visited them when Joe was not around.

Joe could not stop his drinking habit. Maramy also strongly suspected that he was seeing other women. She dared not question him for fear of another flare-up. She found comfort in her children and in the company of Kristina and Ferdie, who both held good jobs. With the money Veronica had bequeathed to Kristina, they were able to afford two cars and a comfortable life.

Kristina and Ferdie often drove Maramy and the children for outings to the park, to fancy malls or to restaurants. They lavished presents on the children, and Maramy and the children were very happy in their company.

Eventually, the children grew into healthy teenagers. Maramy's daughter often told her, "Divorce him. He is awful to you. He is so mean to both of us. At least he is mostly okay with Justin, though. I don't really care about him. For you this is no life."

Maramy's mother was now quite old, and weak and ill. The children did not feel much love for her, but she expected them to visit her often and run errands for her. Maramy persuaded them to come with her whenever she could visit, but they were usually reluctant to do so. "What a pity they are not close to their grandmother," Maramy thought sadly. "If only her mother had shown more warmth and love, they might have gladly reciprocated now."

Then came the crash! The phone was ringing incessantly, and Maramy rushed to answer it. She heard an agitated voice at the other end. "Your husband has met with a serious accident," she was informed. Maramy was given hurried instructions and directions, and she grabbed the children, who had just returned from school, and pulled them out of the door. They were all in shock.

They rushed by cab to the scene of the accident. Her husband and another young woman were being carried into the ambulance. She screamed that she was his wife, and forcibly pushed her way into the ambulance. The children had to come with her as there was no time to call Kristina or her husband, and she had nowhere and nobody to leave them with.

She was given the information that Joe had been completely drunk, and it was he who had caused the accident. Joe died in the ambulance, and the girl died as well, just as they reached the hospital.

Maramy, as usual turned to Kristina for help. "Who was the young woman with Joe?" she wondered. Kristina, after investigating, cleared up that mystery for her. Joe had lived a double life, keeping an apartment for a pretty young girl that he fancied.

This explained his many absences and the smell of perfume on his clothing all these past months.

Kristina and Ferdie made the funeral arrangements. The poor woman who died with Joe did not seem to have any family, as nobody came forward to claim her. Thus it transpired that there were two funerals to arrange.

Maramy was in a daze and completely devastated. Her son was heartbroken. Sadly, her daughter did not seem too upset, and gave her full attention to the needs of her mother in this time of horror and tragedy.

"What would I do without the help of my daughter, Kristina and Ferdie?" Kristina often wondered. "God bless them."

CHAPTER 23

Maramy's mother, now 92 years old, was frightened for her future now that Maramy's husband was no longer around to pay her bills. "Who will pay my rent, food and other comforts?" she wondered. Maramy had also engaged a Filipina girl to be with her during the week, and this was an expensive project. The truth was, Joe had been good to her, though cruel to her daughter. "Will I have to move to Maramy's flat?" she wondered. She felt sure that she would not be as comfortable there as in her own place.

Another shock awaited poor Maramy — she was broke! "Where was Joe's money?" He had always lived an affluent lifestyle, and Maramy had taken it for granted that money was not a problem. She was not able to grasp the fact that he had not left any money, even for his son.

He had evidently spent money as it came in, with no thought of the future. After all, he was still a young man at the time of his sudden death.

Maramy's mother lived another two years with Maramy's help, even though her own finances were now tight. Her mother died in her sleep, completely neglected by her son and his family. She was not greatly grieved for, except by Maramy, who had, after all, lost a mother.

Kristina and Ferdie had been blessed with a son and daughter, and Maramy's daughter Carina, now a beautiful young woman, would often baby-sit for their little ones, who loved her as she loved them. Carina was working to help with finances at home, and also studied at the university. She never complained, was always cheerful, and, unlike her mother, was extremely independent and self-assured.

Maramy had returned to work after Joe's death, though she received a miserly salary for her hard work. Her son was growing up well, and was not at all a problematic teenager. He was also an excellent student at school.

In spite of their different characteristics, Maramy and Carina were very close. Carina possessed Maramy's beauty, but did not have her timidity. Carina was outgoing, self-possessed and ambitious. She knew what she wanted from life, and aimed to achieve her goals. Her father's indifference had not affected her negatively. She was her mother's and brother's protector, and the three of them managed to emerge from the crisis of Joe's sudden death as a caring and happy family.

Carina dated off and on, and tried to encourage Maramy to do the same, with no success. Maramy still carried a torch for Ahmed. "Ahmed, Ahmed!" her heart often cried out. She sometimes wondered if Joe had realized that she did not love him, and wondered if this had caused his cruelty to her. She had tried to be a good wife to Joe, but he had not been easy to live with. Plus, with her heart somewhere else, it was difficult to form a close relationship.

Maramy often looked at her daughter with worry. "What does the future hold for her? Will she also know heartache like me? Will her future be bright and happy, or dismal and sad?" Maramy was comforted by the fact that Carina could take life's knocks on the chin bravely and proudly. In spite of this, her mother prayed that her daughter should be spared pain and hardship, and that she should have a happy future.

Carina found time to go on dates, and Maramy wondered what lucky man would win the heart of her precious daughter. She did not have long to wait. Her question was soon answered.

CHAPTER 24

Though Maramy found her work boring, she had a few co-operative workers and a kind boss. Her boss, Edward Joseph, often looked at his hard-working employee and wondered at her silent reticence and sad eyes. She seemed so unaware of her beauty. She was a hard and smart worker, who never complained; she was an ideal employee.

Edward Joseph had money, position and a lonely heart. A self-made man, he had reached a pinnacle most men would envy. His beloved wife had been ill for quite some time, and had passed away before the tragedy that befell their only son. The boy, on his way to his father's office before returning to his army unit, had been in the bus that was blown up by terrorists.

Many had been killed in this incident, but his son was going through a living death. He had been lying in a coma for years, probably never to waken due to severe brain injuries. Edward Joseph visited his son every day, talking to him, trying to communicate, and never losing hope for a miracle. He never thought for a moment of disconnecting the tubes.

Maramy was the only employee who never failed to ask about his son. She had also visited his son in the nursing home several times, though it was quite a distance away. Mr. Joseph felt her sympathy, and it touched his heart. Maramy seemed unapproachable, and he never let on that his feelings for her were more than deep affection.

Maramy had received many promotions and raises in salary over the years, and was now in charge of the office. Because she was so self-effacing, the other workers had tried to take advantage of her soft nature, but where work was concerned, she had proved herself strong and capable.

One day, Mr. Joseph took it on himself to invite Maramy and her family to his luxurious villa in a fashionable part of town. Maramy gracefully accepted the invitation. She was fond of the elderly man who was so kind and fair to all his employees.

Mr. Joseph sent a car with his personal chauffeur to bring them to his home. Maramy dressed carefully and conservatively, as was her wont.

Carina said to her mother, "I hope we won't be bored. He's an old man and there will be no young people around to talk to."

Justin replied angrily, "We are doing this for mum. Even if the evening is boring, we shouldn't complain."

The villa was impressive. After all, Mr. Joseph was an extremely wealthy man. The table had been laid beautifully, and his personal valet was in charge. Maramy introduced her children to Mr. Joseph, and Justin and Mr. Joseph immediately clicked. Perhaps there was something about the young man that reminded him of his own son. Justin was impressed by the tall, stately man, and they entered into interesting conversations about physics, chemistry, world affairs etc.

Carina could not take her eyes off the many photographs of Mr. Joseph's dead wife that adorned the walls of his home. She was a strikingly beautiful woman with jet-black hair, blue eyes, and a perfect figure. There were photographs everywhere of the husband and wife together, so happy and clearly deeply in love.

"Mr. Joseph," Carina said, "your wife was exceptionally beautiful."

"Thank you, Carina," Mr. Joseph replied. "What was more important than her beauty was that she was good, wise and gentle. She did a great deal of social work and gave much to charity. It makes me bitter to think that she had to suffer so much from her illness, and that she was taken from life at such a young age. Thank goodness, though, she did not live to see our son's tragedy. They adored each other, and I in turn adored them both. I thought myself the happiest man in the world."

Carina glanced at the large photograph of his son in a beautiful gilded frame, and her eyes were full of compassion. "What an extraordinary looking boy, so handsome in his army uniform. I could have fallen for him at first sight if he were here today," Carina thought sadly.

All three enjoyed an excellent meal that was beautifully served. Maramy and her children had put much thought into what they could bring to the house, besides the usual wine and chocolates. With much thought and concentration, they had decided on a beautiful, three-tiered menorah. It was an antique, but shining and polished like new. Mr. Joseph was thrilled with the gift, and the three were filled with gratification for their choice.

On reaching home after an exceptionally pleasant evening, Carina burst out, "What a charming man, mum, I feel he has a soft corner for you."

Maramy blushed. "Don't be foolish. He is just a good boss and a good friend."

Justin was enthusiastic about the meeting, and said to his mother, "I can't wait to meet him again. He knows so much — a walking Google. I have never met such a clever man as Mr. Joseph."

Thus ended a memorable evening that they would never forget.

CHAPTER 25

As time passed, Mr. Joseph and Justin became close. Mr. Joseph had often wondered to whom he would leave his vast fortune. Now that he had become increasingly fond of Justin, and looked on him as the son he had lost, he had an answer. Justin was balm to his grief, and the boy's intelligence and charm were greatly inspiring.

He realized that Justin's mother would never consent to be his wife, and that he should be content to look on her as a dear friend. She was fond of him as a friend, and he realized he would never be more than that to her.

Carina was also affectionate towards him, and looked upon him as the uncle she had never had. Maramy's brother and his family had kept their distance since her father's death, and Carina and Justin did not look upon them as family. They realized that they were looked down upon by that snobbish family, who had risen in life and were always afraid that Maramy or her children would seek their help financially. They did not realize that both Maramy and her children were too proud ever to ask for help financially or otherwise, especially from them.

Maramy's birthday was approaching, and Mr. Joseph had planned a pleasant celebration. He told them that he would pick them up the evening of Maramy's birthday. He had also included Kristina, her husband and their children in his invitation. Kristina said she and her husband would be happy to come, but they would leave their children with a reliable baby-sitter.

Maramy and her children dressed carefully in respect for Mr. Joseph. Carina told her mum, "Wear that slinky blue dress that matches your eyes. It suits you and is also dressy enough for a special occasion."

Maramy complained, "The neckline is too low. That is why I never wear it."

Carina argued, "For an evening occasion a low neckline is an acceptable, and it is not really that low, Mum. Would you wear it to please me?"

Maramy reluctantly consented. Though not in her prime, Maramy looked stunning that evening, and Carina kissed her, saying, "You are the most beautiful mother in the world." Secretly Carina wondered if her mother realized how much Mr. Joseph cared for her, but knew her too well to think the relationship would ever get serious. Besides, in Carina's young eyes Mr. Joseph, who was 30 years her mother's senior, was too old to be a romantic figure.

Mr. Joseph, punctual as usual, arrived in one of his many vans. He drove it himself, as he felt a chauffeur would intrude on the evening. He cut an impressive figure, impeccably dressed in a dark blue suit and matching tie. He was still a very handsome man, dignified and erect. He was an altogether commanding figure.

Mr. Joseph's eyes opened wide when he saw Maramy. She was especially beautiful and radiant this evening. They went off to pick up Kristina and Ferdie. Kristina, as usual, was beautifully dressed and made up, and Ferdie who was seldom seen in a suit, had also worn his best suit and a flashy tie. Their children were not yet asleep, and rushed out to see them off. How they loved Justin and Carina! The love was reciprocal, and it was hard for them to get the children's loving arms gently off their necks, and wish them goodnight.

Mr. Joseph drove for some time, and then stopped just out of town at a beautiful outdoor garden that was large and inviting. Maramy held her breath, as did Kristina, when they recognised this was Ahmed's restaurant, and the place where Maramy had first met him. They both gave silent prayers that they would not see Ahmed there.

Luckily, Mr. Joseph had booked a table in a secluded spot in the garden. Though it was summer, a light breeze played around their shoulders, and the scent of the flowers, especially the roses, was intoxicating.

"What would you like to order?" Mr. Joseph enquired. They all asked him to do the ordering. The waiter, a young, polite Arab boy, took their order in a courteous and pleasant manner, and soon returned with the wine bottles and beautiful wine glasses. Everyone filled their glasses and raised them to drink to Maramy's health and to wish her a wonderful birthday. She blushed and was touched by their affection.

The wine was followed by the most delicious and generous three-course meal they could ever have imagined. The conversation was light and happy, and all were in excellent moods. Suddenly the waiter came to their table with a beautiful three-tiered cake lit with candles. They then sang the "Happy Birthday" song and it brought tears of happiness to Maramy's eyes.

Mr. Joseph produced a small, beautifully wrapped packet from his pocket. "This is your birthday present, dear Maramy," he said. "Please open it."

She did so, and she and all at the table gasped in delight. It was the most exquisite necklace, intricately designed in silver and gold. They all agreed that it was just the thing for Maramy. She was embarrassed, and said to Mr. Joseph, "How can I accept such an expensive gift?"

He told her gently, "Keep it as a remembrance from a good friend."

Maramy, deeply touched, bent over and kissed him on the cheek. "Thank you," she said softly. "I shall always treasure it."

He was pleased, as he had taken much thought and great trouble to find something that would suit Maramy's tender nature. They continued to sit and talk, and he began to reminisce about his younger days as a soldier in the Israeli Army. He also talked about the bitter experiences he had had during his days in the "Hagana" (The first Israeli Defense Force). He had drunk more wine than he was accustomed to, and talked more freely than was his custom. They were fascinated by his stories, especially young Justin, who was more in awe of him than ever.

Carina excused herself from the table, saying she was going to take a look around the beautiful garden with all its special arrangements. By the time they were ready to leave, she had not yet returned. Suddenly Kristina's heart gave a lurch. There was Carina, deep in conversation with a striking-looking Arab youth. Immediately Kristina was struck by his resemblance to Ahmed from so many years ago. Fortunately, Maramy's back was to the scene, so she did not notice. Carina returned in a glowing mood, and they all slowly left the restaurant.

The waiters saluted to Mr. Joseph, whom they seemed to know and respect. In fact, Mr. Joseph had told his friends earlier that this was one of his favorite haunts.

CHAPTER 26

Justin was curious about the connection with Mr. Joseph and his Arab clients and friends. One evening, sitting in Mr. Joseph's beautiful home, his curiosity overcame him. While talking about the general political situation in the country, Justin saw his opening to the subject. "The Arabs are brought up to hate us," he blurted. "Nothing we do can alleviate their hate."

Mr. Joseph looked at Justin with concentration. Then he gently replied to Justin, "You see, Justin, I can also hate them and blame them for destroying my son's future and his life. I can blame them for my son's awful condition, their action that has robbed me of any future happiness or plans. However, Justin, I have learned not to blame all for the deeds of some," he said as a tear glistened like a shining diamond and trickled down his strong-featured face.

Justin was shocked and hurt to see his pain. Mr. Joseph continued, "I grew up in a poor neighbourhood in Jaffa. We had many Arab neighbors, and there was a lot of friendship and even affection among us. When my father died quite suddenly, our Arab friends rallied around us, bringing food, comfort and sympathy. I can never forget that. I have had business relations and also many friends among the Arab community, and have never been let down yet.

"My dear friend, Ahmed, the owner of the restaurant I took you all to on your mum's birthday, has been a close friend for many years. I cannot and never will condone the terrorists and the militant groups' behavior. It is because of them that my son's life has been shortened, and my hopes for him crushed. Sadly, there are many others like him. "

"One of my workers has had the same experience with his son lying in a coma for years. Ask your mother. She knows about that. His father is bitter and angry, and talks against the Arabs all the time. But to condemn my good friends just because they are Arabs is not fair to them or to my principles. Like all of us, I pray for peace and hope that one day we can live side by side as friends. Hopefully that will happen, one day!"

This was a long speech for Mr. Joseph, and Justin was surprised, as Mr. Joseph was usually a man of few words. He was now able to see Mr. Joseph's side of the picture, and admired him tremendously for not allowing feelings of hate to cause destruction in his relationships.

Justin was to enter the Army soon, and his conscription bothered him. At home he was gentle and kind, but knew that he would have to learn to be hard, and maybe even cruel sometimes. He also knew that his mother worried more and more as his conscription date drew closer. He ached for her, and wanted to spare her the fear and worry, but this situation was unavoidable. He knew he had to give three years of his life willingly to do service for his country.

There were times when he felt a void and still missed his father. He wondered how his father had dealt with the army and the wars he had been through, and if this had perhaps contributed to his harshness and escape in drink. His father was dead, though, and he would never know the answers.

Maramy, for her part, often thought of her dead husband. "Maybe he felt I did not really love him, and this made him take to drink and run after other women? Maybe the death of his mother at a young age inflicted a pain that he needed to reflect?" There were nights when she would wake up in a cold sweat, seeing his face before her, his manner and expression threatening.

One night Carina rushed into her room, frightened and worried. "Mum, what's the matter? I was awakened by your screams!"

"It must have been a bad dream, Carina," her mother answered, her voice still shaking. "Go back to sleep," she said, trying to soothe her daughter's fear for her.

Maramy had worked hard, and received a good wage. She had tried to meet all her children's needs and requirements, both mental and physical. However, her hours at work and commuting to and from work took up most of her time. Her only relaxation was being at home with her children, or visiting Kristina and her family, who also came to visit often.

She and Kristina had remained close friends, and Kristina's husband was included in the meetings, as were the children. Kristina's children were older now, but still looked up to Justin and Carina, who also loved them very much.

Maramy was now able to move to a larger, more comfortable home. It had a small garden, and a parking space for Carina's car. After her husband's death and the financial chaos that had ensued; she had been forced to move to a tiny, much cheaper apartment. Now they were in a better area and a bigger house.

Mr. Joseph was their kind godfather, and Kristina was their fairy princess who, together with her husband and children, filled the gap of family life that they so sorely missed.

At last Maramy felt contentment, taking pride in her children and her beautiful home. Life was looking up for her.

CHAPTER 27

Maramy had noticed that Carina took special care of her make-up and dress lately, and looked especially glamorous and glowing. She had also begun to come home later, with no explanation to her mother of where she had gone or who she had met. "Should I keep quiet or push the button by confronting her about her unusual behaviour?" she asked herself. Maramy decided to talk to her dear friend Kristina and ask her advice about how to approach her daughter about what was going on.

"Kristina will be home now," Maramy thought. She picked up the receiver and dialed Kristina's number. "Hello, Kristina," she said in her soft gentle voice. "I have a problem and need your help and advice. Carina has distanced herself from me and I cannot understand why.

She often comes home late, and doesn't confide in me anymore. This hurts. What would you advise me to do? I'd like to hear your viewpoint as you are always so right!"

Kristina had had her own suspicions about what was going on, but did not let Maramy have an inkling of this. "Don't worry, Maramy dear," she said. I will diplomatically try to find out from Carina what is going on in her life just now. Give me time and I will get back to you with an answer."

"Oh, thank you Kristina. You are really one in a million. I am lucky to have you as a friend," Maramy said gratefully.

"I am lucky, too, to have you as a friend," Kristina said. "Bye, and we'll talk again soon."

Kristina made an appointment to meet Carina after work. They had always been close, and Carina loved meeting with Kristina, who was always lively, optimistic, and patient with modern views of the new generation. That evening they met at their favourite little Italian restaurant. Kristina noticed that Carina really was glowing and in a happy mood. "Carina, you look lovely," Kristina said to her. "What's up? What's the latest news?" she continued.

"Oh, Kristina dear, I have wonderful news for you. I am in love! Really in love with a wonderful man who is everything a girl could wish for."

"Who is the lucky man?" Kristina asked her curiously.

"There is a snag, unfortunately," Carina said in a softer and more subdued tone. "The man I love and who loves me is an Arab."

Kristina was shocked. "Is history repeating itself?" she asked herself.

There was silence for a few minutes. Carina watched her anxiously. Kristina had always been there for her, as her champion and her confidante. Next to her mother and brother, she loved and adored Kristina and her family most.

Kristina, seeing Carina's worried look, pulled herself together. She smiled broadly and said, "You're in love! Let's celebrate. Love calls for a special celebration!" The waiter was at their table, and she ordered the best and most expensive cake on the menu, together with her favorite steaming cappuccino coffee. Neither drank any form of alcohol, so wine was not ordered.

Carina felt a wave of relief. "Thank G-d for Kristina," she thought. Her own mother had more rigid views on life, and she had not dared to tell her that her new boyfriend was an Arab.

After chatting for a while about work and other general subjects. Kristina asked Carina, "Shall I break the news gently to your mother?"

"Please do, Kristina, and I am sure you will speak up for me," Carina answered gratefully. "I don't want to hide anything from her. As you know, I love her dearly, but I have been afraid to hurt her in any way. I know she would be upset at the news that I am seeing an Arab."

"How ironic!" Kristina thought, remembering how Maramy had gone through the same experience, which of course Carina knew nothing about. "I hope this time the ending will be happier," Kristina thought. She hurt for Carina, knowing this relationship would not be easy, and fearing that history could repeat itself. She never wanted to see Carina hurt as her mother had been.

Carina was clearly very worried about her mother's reaction. "She is so tender and frail. She will surely be against this relationship. Maybe she will associate him with terrorists, though he is very well-educated, liberal minded and works as a doctor in an Israeli hospital. He is gorgeous, Kristina! You will love him. He is also charming, kind, clever and gentle."

"I'm sure we will get on well," Kristina assured her, though in her heart she was not so sure.

Carina thanked Kristina profusely for reassuring her and in general for being there for her. They kissed and parted.

CHAPTER 28

Kristina spoke to Maramy the next day. She did not confirm the identity of Carina's new friend, but advised Maramy to be patient and accepting when Carina confided in her. She simultaneously told Carina that it was time she confided in her mum, as she had already prepared the groundwork for Carina.

One evening, Carina came home smiling and happy. "I have met a wonderful guy!" she told her mum. "This time it's serious. You will love him, mum. He is a good man, and I know I will be happy with him."

Maramy did not press the point, as she wanted Carina to tell her of her own accord. She hugged Carina and said gently, "I hope you will be happy. I am so glad to see you in this joyous mood."

It took Carina a few days to confirm the identity of her new boyfriend. She was anxious to tell her, but Kristina had cautioned her to break the news slowly. Carina tried to be as tactful as possible, telling her mother that she was in love with a doctor, and that Maramy would surely love him. Only then did she say to her mother, "He is not Jewish. He is a Muslim. But he is a wonderful human being, and that's what counts. Doesn't it, mum?"

Maramy, in her gentle way, tried to convince Carina that this was the wrong choice. "An Arab? It would be dangerous for you to be affiliated with an Arab, let alone think of marrying him," she explained. In her heart she wondered if she should relate to Carina the story of her old romance from so many years ago, and the misery and shock of rejection that had affected her all these years.

Carina told her mother enthusiastically, "You must meet him and judge for yourself. He is honest, kind and reliable, and you will love him as I do. You will be glad of my choice, even though he is a different religion."

After Carina's and Kristina's persistent persuasion, Maramy reluctantly agreed to meet the man of her daughter's dreams. She was still worried that her daughter would experience the same pain and rejection that she had endured and never really recovered from.

The meeting was arranged in Kristina's home. Maramy dressed with extra care, and together with her son and daughter went in Carina's car to meet the young man.

Kristina and Ferdie's young children rushed up to them when they reached Kristina's home, hugging them and chattering at the same time. They loved Maramy and her children, and were always happy to see Carina and Justin.

As they entered, Kristina came running and hugged Maramy, holding her hand tightly. She knew Maramy was in for a shock — the same shock she had experienced when she first set eyes on Carina's young man.

When he came to stand before them, Maramy nearly fainted. Here before her was the spitting image of Ahmed, her first and only sweetheart. This was a young man, and Ahmed had also been young when she had last seen him. Maramy was in complete shock.

CHAPTER 29

Carina introduced him, and he seemed shy, and possibly worried about their reaction to him being a Muslim. They talked for a while, and then Maramy, pleading a severe headache, asked to be excused so she could go home and rest.

"Can we meet again soon?" he asked politely.

"Yes, yes," Maramy forced herself to say in a warm and friendly way, not wanting to completely disappoint her daughter.

"Can we arrange that you come to my house next? On Monday? All of you are invited," he said, nodding to Kristina and her husband as well.

Kristina was disappointed. She had prepared a fine table, and all Maramy had before preparing to leave was a cup of tea and a biscuit. Kristina took down the address of their next meeting, and it was arranged that they would meet there at 5 p.m. the following Monday.

Carina tried to hide her disappointment at her mother's reaction, but hoped their next meeting would be more successful. She reluctantly said goodbye and they left after asking Kristina to excuse their having to leave so soon.

Maramy knew that both her children were at a loss to understand why she needed to leave in such a hurry. She apologized to them and said the next meeting would be better.

The days flew by, and as planned, they were on their way to the address Kristina had written down. She would be going there directly with her husband and children.

They arrived at a magnificent, palatial home. "This guy of yours must be rolling in wealth!" Justin said jokingly to his sister.

"It is the first time I have come here," she said. "I am impressed."

They were escorted to a large and spacious hall by a manservant. Everything was decorated in good taste, and the atmosphere was warm and welcoming. The young man came forward and shook their hands, rumpling the hair of Kristina's two young children affectionately. He was immaculately dressed, and looked like he had come out of a fashion magazine. Indeed, he was so striking that he could have passed for a model.

"Ahmed!" Maramy thought. "Ahmed, am I looking at you again?"

Her heart wrenched, but she shook the young man's hand warmly, trying to make up for her abrupt departure at their last meeting.

They were seated soon after, and Kristina, good friend that she was, made it a point to sit as close as possible to Maramy, knowing she would need moral support.

Justin looked longingly at the well-laid table. He could see all his favorite Arab sweets, plus delicious looking cakes, salads and goodies of all sorts. He was thirsty, and could see there was an assortment of drinks on the table. He had often eaten at Mr. Joseph's place, and was familiar with the Arab sweets that both he and Mr. Joseph enjoyed immensely. Suddenly, he wished that Mr. Joseph were here with them. He loved the man and looked on him as family, even a father figure.

"My father will be here soon," the young man said.

"What about your mother?" Kristina asked.

"She passed away when I was young," he answered. "She had been ill for a long time. My father never married again. I am an only child, and my father and I are very close."

Maramy steeled herself for what was to come. She was now able to understand the situation better. This young man could only be Ahmed's son. The resemblance was so great that there could be no other explanation.

She was right. As they were seated in the plush, comfortable armchairs in the spacious and beautiful living room, a tall, impressive man entered. It was her Ahmed, only much older now. His hair was silver, his face more lined.

CHAPTER 30

Maramy's heart jumped as Ahmed looked keenly at her. His eyes were moist, and his face was glowing with joy at seeing her again.

Kristina broke the ice. "We know each other," she explained to Carina. "At least, your mother and I knew Ahmed many years ago."

"Yes," Ahmed said. "We go a back a long way."

Carina was delighted. "Oh, you knew each other? That's wonderful, isn't it?" she exclaimed happily, turning to her love, Imaram. He smiled understandingly. Carina had the feeling that he knew more than he let on.

Maramy felt ill. "How could he dare to face me after letting me down so badly years ago?" she thought. She was cold and indifferent to Ahmed. Carina noticed and wondered at the change in her mother who was usually so warm and friendly.

Kristina, realizing her friend's discomfiture and anger, moved beside her and pressed her hand. Maramy's hand was cold and clammy. "What Fate has brought us together after all these years?" she mused.

Ahmed offered to take Ferdie on a tour of his large estate and asked Justin if he would like to see the grounds and the stables. Justin jumped with alacrity at the opportunity, He loved horses, and had often visited Mr. Joseph's stable full of well bred steeds.

Carina and Imaram also decided to go for a walk outside, so Kristina and Maramy were left alone. The two women looked at each other. Kristina was heartbroken to see the tears and sadness in her friend's eyes. Kristina spoke softly and consolingly to Maramy, "Try not to be too hard on him. Not only for his, but also for the sake of your children. Carina seems to be very much in love, and Imaram clearly adores her. Ahmed has probably suffered a great deal for his mistake in giving you up. It must have caused him great pain."

"What about my pain? Maramy quickly replied. "What about my suffering all these years, and the years I wasted marrying on the rebound and then living with a cruel and unloving man? My love for Ahmed ruined my life!"

"You have two wonderful children," Kristina answered. "Count your blessings. Don't allow your daughter's life to be prejudiced by your hurt and ruined like yours was."

For a time they sat silently in contemplation. "How will I explain matters to Carina?" Maramy thought sadly. "What a coincidence meeting Ahmed again after all these years and seeing my daughter and his son so much in love. What stand should I take now? I can never forgive Ahmed for jilting me. The shock he put me through! I was ready to give up all for him. He left me and never looked back. Never thought twice about my suffering!"

Kristina also was deep in thought. "How can I convince Maramy to forgive him? She is so beautiful still. She has rejected all her suitors since she was widowed. I am sure that Mr. Joseph, though older, would have loved to have her as his wife. I wonder if she has been carrying a torch for Ahmed all these years. She is obviously in pain. I hope she won't throw him out of her life if he wants to be a part of it now. Surely she won't, when her daughter and his son are so entwined in their love."

CHAPTER 31

Carina and Imaram came in, glowing, holding hands, their faces shining with love for each other. Carina had told her mother that her new boyfriend and she were compatible, and could talk for hours on subjects of mutual interest. "I was ready to marry a man not of my faith," Maramy thought. "Can I blame Carina for accepting Imaram in spite of his religion, and loving and respecting him regardless of possible consequences?"

Ahmed, Ferdie and Justin also returned from their stroll and Imaram went up to his father, saying. "We are planning to get married soon, Dad. Do we have your blessing?"

"You have my blessing," Ahmed answered warmly. "I will support you and Carina in every way I can. I am happy with your choice of a wife, and thrilled to be gaining a lovely daughter."

He turned to Maramy as she sat looking stone-faced and asked, "How do you feel about this marriage?"

"Whatever they wish," she answered diffidently.

"You do not sound very enthusiastic," Ahmed said.

"Do you expect me to act differently?" she answered bitterly.

Pain crossed Ahmed's handsome face. "I made a grave mistake once, and how I have suffered for it. Today I shall see that my son does not make the same mistake. Besides, he is more clear-headed than I was, so I know he won't. I don't have to worry. Imaram is strong-minded and will not be swayed by the wishes of others. I admire his decisive mind, and I can vouch for his integrity. I know he will make an excellent and devoted husband to Carina. I have complete faith in him."

"Do you have the same confidence in yourself?" Maramy asked him sharply.

He did not answer.

Carina looked perturbed. "What's the matter, mum?" she asked worriedly.

"Nothing," Maramy quietly answered. "Kristina, I want to go home," Maramy said, turning to her friend.

Kristina saw the determination on her friend's face and did not think it wise to dissuade her. They politely said their goodbyes.

Carina was quiet on the way home, but upon entering the house she asked her mother in a concerned voice, "What's the matter, mum? You were in such a hurry to leave that it seemed almost rude."

"No, no," Maramy replied quickly. "I was preoccupied. I worry about your future. You will be going far from me with a man of another faith."

"I have full trust in him," Carina told her mother curtly.

CHAPTER 32

The wedding day was arranged. Maramy, seeing she could not confide her fears even to Kristina, who seemed all for the wedding, turned to Mr. Joseph, her friend and mentor. "Mr. Joseph," she said worriedly, "what shall I do? Shall I try to stop it?"

His answer stunned her. He was positive about the marriage and did not hesitate to put an end to her fears. "I have known the family for years. I can vouch for them wholeheartedly. They are my close and trustworthy friends. Carina could not make a better match."

"But he is a Muslim," she argued.

"So what?" Mr. Joseph answered with a smile. "I have many Jewish friends who have married Muslims, Jewish women who are happy with their choice of a Muslim husband. It depends on the character of a man and woman, and you know you do not have to doubt the character of either of these two well-educated, fully aware, young persons.

"I have known Imaram since he was born. I knew his mother, and his father is and has always been, a close friend. Don't worry, this marriage will work out very well and you will be pleased with your daughter's choice, I assure you."

When the wedding day arrived, it was sunny, and cloudless, with blue skies and warm, comforting weather.

Carina, wearing a beautiful white lace dress, was amazingly lovely, and Imaram was strikingly handsome in a well-cut navy blue suit and a matching tie. They were an interesting looking pair, a blonde beauty and an Eastern-looking, dark-haired young man — the contrast was perfect. What a picture they made together.

In spite of her qualms, Maramy was proud of her daughter's beauty and confidence. There were many photographs taken.

Justin was also justly proud of his sister. He and Imaram had got on famously from the beginning, and found many mutual topics of interest.

The food was beautifully displayed and very tasty, and the wine was the best. The hall had been decorated with balloons, and flower arrangements were artistically placed on tables and around the room. Above was a huge chandelier that threw a warm light on all below.

Mr. Joseph rose to toast the happy couple. His speech was short, and his voice melodious. There was pin-drop silence as he spoke. "I have known this couple well, and I foresee a wonderful future for them. They are most suitable to each other. Both come from good homes and both are well-educated. They love each other deeply and I, like them, am sure of their brilliant future. Let us all drink a toast to the happiness of the bride and groom, and wish them many loving and joyous years together." Everyone clapped, and all were struck by the strong and positive personality of this man, who, though a millionaire, was humble, kind, and extremely charming.

"We are all lucky to have him as our friend," Maramy whispered to Kristina, who agreed heartily. Maramy and Kristina were resplendent in their choice of beautiful clothes. They both looked fashionably lovely. Kristina's husband, who had become good friends with Ahmed, kept himself busy looking after his two smartly dressed children, keeping them in check. In fact, they were not their usual mischievous selves, but very solemn and serious.

CHAPTER 33

The marriage had taken place in the civil office, and the party was later held in Ahmed's luxurious restaurant. "Who will run the restaurant when Imaram leaves?" Kristina wondered.

Ahmed, the proud father of the bridegroom, himself a striking figure, came up to Kristina and asked politely, "May I have a few words with you?"

"Of course," Kristina answered. They moved to a quiet corner. Kristina had since given up on her misgivings about Ahmed and the hurt he had caused her friend, though she still kept her distance.

"You should know, Kristina, that I have always loved Maramy," he said. "I thought she might not be happy with me being of a different faith. I was young and afraid of my family's reaction. They might not have accepted her, or in the least, would have expected her to convert. I was also a devoted Muslim at the time. I know I was a coward not to face my parents, because today I realize that it would not have been so terrible after all. They would have put my happiness first."

"Kristina, please try to persuade Maramy to trust me again. I know now that it is the person that counts. Love, a kind heart, good actions are of greater importance than all religious beliefs. Good words, good thoughts, good deeds, that is what every religion advocates. I wish I knew then what I know now."

"I beg you, plead for me to Maramy. I have never stopped loving her. My wife and I had a good marriage, though it was arranged, but I never stopped loving Maramy and thinking of her. I even named my only son after her. See, spell Imaram backwards, and what do you get? Maramy. While I never forsook my wife or betrayed her in the few years we had together, and I think she was happy with me, I never stopped thinking of Maramy. "

"My love for Maramy is deep and true. She has never left my heart. Please, please, plead my case, I beg of you, Kristina!"

Kristina, deeply moved by the pain and passion in his voice, pressed his palm in sympathy.

Kristina spoke to Maramy every day, trying to persuade her to give Ahmed another chance. He, on his side of things, kept phoning Maramy daily, sending her flowers, and begging her to meet with him.

The day came for Imaram and Carina to leave for their new life abroad. Carina looked at her mother and brother with tears in her eyes. Kristina and Ferdie were also present with their two children, as was Mr. Joseph, who had also come to see them off.

Carina bent and whispered in her mother's ear. "Darling mum. I know it all now. Ahmed loves you and always has. I know that you love him, too. He made a mistake when he rejected you. Forgive him, mum. You deserve every happiness. Do it for my sake, I implore you!"

Maramy looked at Ahmed. The love and adoration in his eyes as he looked at her could not be mistaken.

They all waved goodbye to Carina and Imaram, as they watched them go, walking arm-in-arm.

Maramy began to cry, but felt a strong arm supporting her. It was not her son, who had turned to Ferdie and Mr. Joseph, trying to hide his pain at Carina's leaving to go so far away. It was Ahmed who drew her to his side, stroking her hair and whispering words of encouragement and love.

Maramy suddenly knew her ordeal was over. She loved and was loved by a good man, whose tenderness and loving kindness would carry her safely through the years.

Love had conquered all!

9 781604 148862